Supporting Learning in Schools

For Tasmin,
all the way away in Kirriemuir!
KMcC

This is a ... ts are either
the pr... titiously.

Text © 2005 Karen McCombie
Illustrations © 2005 Lydia Monks

The right of Karen McCombie and Lydia Monks to be identified as author
and illustrator respectively of this work has been asserted by them in accordance
with the Copyright, Designs and Patents Act 1988

This book has been typeset in Granjon

Printed and bound in Great Britain by
Creative Print and Design (Wales), Ebbw Vale

British Library Cataloguing in Publication Data:
a catalogue record for this book is available from the British Library

ISBN 978-1-4063-0719-1

www.walkerbooks.co.uk

Being Grown-up is Cool (Not!)

KAREN McCOMBIE

LYDIA MONKS

AND SUBSIDIARIES

LONDON · BOSTON · SYDNEY · AUCKLAND

Being bored is dangerous

I was a bit bored.

OK, I was a

LOT

bored.

Which is why I'd spent twenty minutes in Caitlin's bedroom, gawping at all her amazing clothes, flicking through her piles of magazines and sniffing all of her perfumes and body sprays.

I *knew* Caitlin wouldn't mind me being in her room. And I *knew* she wouldn't mind me gawping, flicking through and sniffing at her stuff, as she is very cool that way.

Apart from being cool, here are

TEN THINGS YOU NEED TO KNOW ABOUT CAITLIN:

1 She is our lodger. (Which means she rents the spare room from Mum. And me, I guess, since this is where I live too.)

2 She is nineteen.

3 She is Scottish.

4 She is a nanny. (Except she keeps getting sacked from her nannying jobs, which is handy for Mum, as it means Caitlin can babysit

8

for me when Mum's at work.)

5 She has a pierced nose
and interesting hair.

6 She plays the didgeridoo.
(If you don't know what one
of those is, think of a **HUGE**
hollow stick that makes a
boomy, burping sort of noise
when you blow into it.)

7 She's painted her room deep purple,
and has silver and black curtains.

8 You can hardly see the deep
purple walls 'cause of all the
posters she's stuck up.

9 She has **FIVE** pairs of
platform trainers, in
FIVE different colours.

10 She's a bit smelly.

OK, so the last one's not true.

But Caitlin must *think* she's very smelly, if she needs all those perfumes and body sprays that are cluttering up her dressing table…

Anyway, it was nearly tea-time, and – like I said – I was bored.

I'd had a pretty nice time round at my dad's earlier. Because it had been a really rainy Sunday afternoon, me and Dylan (my step-brother) and Fiona (my step-mum) and Dad (my, er, dad) had played five games of Mousetrap in a row, and I'd won four of them (hurray!).

Then I came home and Mum was busy with boring work stuff, and our three dogs were all snuggled and snoozly by the radiators and didn't want to go out for a walk (boring), and everything on TV was boring, and Caitlin was out at the movies, so I couldn't talk to her about non-boring things, and I was just plain

BORRRREEEEDDDD!!!

Suddenly, Mum shouted through that tea was ready, so I put the perfume bottle I was sniffing back down on the dressing table and stood up to go.

Only I didn't get very far.

"whooooooooaaaaaaah!!!"
THUD!!

The **"whooooooooaaaaaaah!!!"** thing? Well, that was me doing a **wobbly** windmill impression. I'd kind of forgotten

that I'd tried on Caitlin's cherry-red platform train-ers, and it took a minute of flapping my arms in wild circles to get my balance and not fall over.

Then **THUD!!**, I fell over – over Dibbles the dog, who must have ambled in and fallen asleep by my feet when I wasn't looking.

It took another minute to scrape myself off the carpet, check Dibbles wasn't squashed, and put the trainers back where I found them.

"Uh, hi," I tried to say casually, when I finally got to the kitchen two minutes and a lot of flustering later.

I expected Mum to ask what the **"whoooaaaah!!!"** and **THUD!!** had been about, but she didn't.

I was quite chuffed about this, as I knew Mum wouldn't really be thrilled about me noseying around Caitlin's room on my own. Thank goodness there was no way she could know about me trying on Caitlin's shoes and stuff – she'd be *really* cross with me then…

"Sorry, babes…" Mum muttered instead, plonking a sandwich in front of me. "Got a lot of, erm, homework to do

tonight, and didn't have time to cook you anything."

"That's OK," I said with a shrug, eyeing up two squint slabs of bread with lettuce sticking out like a frilly tutu in the middle. "What's your homework?"

"Hmmm?"

"Is it more about how to look after tree frogs?"

"*Hmmm?*" Mum *hmmed* again, not really listening to me.

"I SAID, ARE YOU READING MORE ABOUT TREE FROGS?"

Mum is the Assistant Manager of the Paws For Thought Animal Rescue Centre. This week, they rescued three tree frogs (very cute; very green; very small). This was good news for the tree frogs, but tricky for Mum and everyone at the centre 'cause they hadn't a clue how to look after them. In fact, Mum had to phone

The Society of People Who Like To Keep WEIRD Pets

(or something) and find out what kind of frogs they were in the first place.

And now they were temporarily living with us, till they felt a bit more happy and hoppy.

"No, it's not about frogs," Mum mumbled, flicking through a bunch of notes. "This is just other ... stuff."

I was about to ask what sort of stuff it was when I started wondering what my frilly sandwich was exactly.

"*Just* lettuce?" I asked in surprise, lifting the top squint slice of bread.

"What?" said Mum, glancing up from her secret home-work and frowning.

"But where's the tuna?"

"I dunno," I muttered, wondering if she might want me to check my pockets or something. "Still swimming in the sea, maybe?"

"Oh, I'm sorry, Indie," Mum said, rubbing a hand through her messy blonde hair and making it look even more messy. "I *meant* to make you a tuna salad sandwich…

I must have got muddled, because I was thinking about all of **this**."

She waved some sheets of paper in front of her.

"That's OK," I told her, not really bothered about her ditziness (I was *totally* used to it). "But what is all **that**?"

"Hmmm?"

I *really* wished Mum would stop with the *hmmms* and maybe just listen to me for five seconds, especially when I was trying to be interested in her job.

"Um … nothing for you to worry about, Indie."

"What do you mean, it's nothing for me to worry about?" I asked, feeling worried now.

"Look, I didn't *mean* it like that," Mum said, sounding ever so slightly irritated. "It's just work stuff."

Now I was ever so slightly irritated too. It was funny, but my normally v. nice mum had been a bit grouchy and grumpy over the last few days. And usually she'd never talk to me in that *I'm-a-grown-up, you're-a-kid- and-wouldn't-understand* way.

I mean, I could understand most things, even BIG complicated things like people getting divorced (ie Mum and Dad), and people not having as much money as other people (ie Mum and my friends' families), and people having to work very hard and get lodgers in (ie Mum and Caitlin).

So why was Mum suddenly talking to me like I was a baby? She'd done that a few times over the last couple of days…

What was up with her?

Y'know, at times like this, I couldn't wait to be a grown-up too. At least I'd get treated as if I had a brain!

"INDIA…?!"

Uh-oh. When Mum spoke just then I jumped – she hardly *ever* uses my proper whole first name.

"What?"

Double uh-oh.

She was staring hard –
really hard –
at me.

"Where on *earth* has half your left eyebrow gone?!"

Uh-oh, uh-oh, uh-oh…

"India … what have you been up to?"

"I just tried some of Caitlin's face cream, that's all!" I squeaked, as Mum came

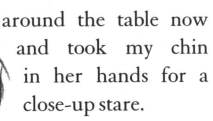

around the table now and took my chin in her hands for a close-up stare.

HELP. I didn't think anyone would notice or mind if I rubbed just a weeny little bit of Caitlin's moisturiser on my face. How could that make half my left eyebrow disappear?

"India, *which* cream did you use?" Mum said urgently. "Can you remember what it looked like?"

"It—it was in a sort of pink tube," I mumbled some more. "It didn't smell very nice…"

"Oh, Indie! I think that might have been hair-removing cream, you silly sausage!"

Hmm, I guess being bored can sometimes be dangerous.

And I guess – considering that Mum was looking stern *and* rolling her eyes at the same time – that it would be quite a while before she started treating me like a grown-up.

Drat…

2

Two eyebrows are better than one

Mum sat on the edge of the bath, tutting at the tube in her hands, as if she was trying to figure out how her daughter got to be so dumb.

While she was busy tutting, I decided that being ten years old really sucked.

At least when you're a grown-up, people don't go around telling you off like a bossy-boots teacher…

"You know, I really can't believe you did this, Indie," sighed Mum.

OK, so two eyebrows are better than one, but did Mum have to make me feel so much of a dorky little kid?

"But I didn't know it was hair-removing cream!" I muttered from behind the soapy face cloth. (Mum had told me to wash my face, to get rid of all traces of hair-removing cream, before any more of my eyebrow started disappearing.)

"Indie, for a girl who **zoomed** through all the Harry Potter books with no problem, I'd have thought you'd have managed to read a couple of simple words on a tube!" she said, reaching over and handing me a towel now.

"Look, I thought it was just moisturiser!" I tried to tell Mum (*again*).

"Indie," Mum sighed *(again)*, "it doesn't matter whether it was normal face cream, or hair-removing cream, or magic cream that makes you invisible. The point is, you shouldn't rummage about in anyone's things without checking with them first. It's not very nice, is it?"

"Caitlin *wasn't* around to ask! And anyway, I knew she wouldn't mind," I muttered, too scared to look in the mirror again and see my WEIRD, semi-missing eyebrow.

"India, Caitlin is a guest in this house, and our friend. What you did was very rude. And silly."

Y'know, I really loved my mum, but she was acting like

a . . .

a . . .

mum,
making me feel like a
complete
baby.

ga ga!

"Hiya!"
said someone at
the bathroom door, who

Hiya!

just happened to be Caitlin.
I hadn't realized she'd
come in – the dogs were
obviously too sleepy and
lazy to bark her hello.
She was looking v.v.v. cool today, I
noticed. She'd tied her hair into loads of
tight bobbles over her head, had a new,
twinkly stone in her pierced nose, a T-shirt
that said,

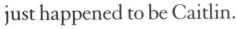

'I'M SHY BUT NOBODY KNOWS IT'

in huge letters, a tartan mini-kilt, *and* a purple pair of her chunky, big trainers.

"Hi! How was the movie you went to see this afternoon?" I blurted out quickly, hoping Caitlin wouldn't ask what was going on, since the answer would be way too embarrassing.

"Yeah, it was good," Caitlin nodded. "It was about these mutant dinosaurs from space who try to take over the world and eat half of Texas."

"Wow..." I mumbled, thinking how much cooler and grown-up that sounded than winning four games of Mousetrap in a row and accidentally making half your eyebrow disappear.

"So … what's going on with you guys?" Caitlin suddenly asked, sending my heart slip-sliding to the floor with a **ker-thump.**

"Indie, are YOU going to tell Caitlin, or will I?"

Mum's (two matching) eyebrows were raised as she spoke, as if she was asking a question, except it was an order really.

"Sorry-Caitlin-I-sort-of-used-some-of-your-stuff…" The words tumbled out in an embarrassed jumble, and now I didn't dare look Caitlin in the eyes.

"Huh? What stuff?" I heard her ask.

Caitlin sounded curious, but not annoyed or anything.

So I peeked up at her – and saw that she was blowing a **ginormous** pink bubble of gum.

"Um … I tried your moisturiser out, only it wasn't moisturiser," I waffled – while Mum held up the tube of hair-remover as evidence of my dumbness.

"Oops," said Caitlin, sucking her pink bubblegum back in. "If it makes you feel any better, kid, I once got hold of my dad's electric razor and accidentally shaved a big chunk of hair off right above my ear."

"Oh, dear!" gasped Mum. "But I bet

you were just a little girl when you did that. Indie's ten and should really know better."

"No – I was seventeen," said Caitlin, leaning casually on the doorframe and blowing another mega pink bubble of gum, and sucking it right back in again.

"Really?" Mum said with a frown. "Well, anyway, I think that Indie owes you an apology – not just for using your things, but for going into your room without permission."

"Uh, yeah, sorry…" I muttered on cue.

"Whatever," said Caitlin with a shrug. "As long as you don't doodle dumb stuff all over my posters, Indie, it doesn't bother me!"

Yay for Caitlin!

She didn't act like a mum or a bossy-boots teacher. She was a grown-up, but she was funny and laidback and cool.

It was then that I decided it was time for a new project: I was going to try and act like a cool grown-up too – and Caitlin could be my inspiration.

And first, I'd have to go and buy myself some gum and practise blowing

BIG,
pink
bubbles…

3
The list of grown-up -ness

I like doing projects.

Not the sort you sometimes do at school, like **'Why The Dinosaurs Disappeared'.** (By the way, I think it was 'cause they ate each other. They're always eating each other on TV shows.)

No, I like doing cool projects. For my first project, I had to think up things I could be good at (turned out I was good at finding a home for an ugly dog at Mum's rescue centre – Dibbles moved in with us).

For my second project, I had to help find some best friends for my step-brother Dylan (his new best friends turned out to be me, and my mates Soph and Fee).

Anyway, it was Monday, and I was round at Soph's house after school, busy telling Dylan, Soph and Fee about my brand new project...

"I want to be more like a grown-up. A really – *gulp* – cool grown-up," I mumbled, finding it kind of hard to talk and chew a big wodge of bubblegum at the same time. "Like Caitlin."

"Why?" asked Dylan, perching on Soph's bed and boinging a neon yo-yo up and down.

"I'll read you this list I've started writing, then – *gulp* – you'll see why."

"No, Indie," he said. "I mean, why are you chewing gum? You never chew gum!"

"Well, I do – *gulp* – now, OK?"

Dylan often asks questions you don't expect. Which makes them really hard to answer.

"What's on your list, Indie?" asked Fee, as she snuggled an armful of Soph's Beanies.

"I've only got three – *gulp* – things so far," I began. "It goes like this…

BEING GROWN-UP IS COOL
1 You're treated as if you've got a **BRAIN**.

"Who treats you like you haven't got a brain?" Fee interrupted.

"My mum," I told her. "She—"

Oops. I nearly launched right into how much of a dork Mum had made me feel over the half-an-eyebrow thing. But I didn't want to do that — it was way too embarrassing and not very grown-up at all.

"Er, she's gone all *weird* and grouchy on me the last few days," I said instead, stroking the long piece of hair I'd combed over one side of my face.

"*Your* mum? But *your* mum is always dead nice!" Soph said in surprise.

"Yeah, well you haven't had her telling you off like you're five years old lately! And that's what's next on my **BEING GROWN-UP IS COOL** list:

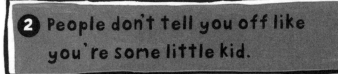

2 People don't tell you off like you're some little kid.

"Yeah, but what's your mum been

telling you off for, Indie?" Fee interrupted again.

Great – another tricky question.

"Just … *everything*," I said vaguely, stroking the long piece of hair again.

I was so, so glad that Caitlin had come up with the idea of me brushing a bit of my hair over like this – neither of my friends or Dylan had noticed my eyebrow (or lack of it). It obviously *wasn't* too different from my usual hairstyle for anyone to make a big deal of it.

"Why have you done your hair like that, Indie?" said Dylan suddenly.

Sigh.

Dylan *would* have to say something.

"Done my hair like what?" I mumbled with a shrug. "It's just in two bunches, just like normal!"

"No, it's not! Why have you combed that one long bit over your face?" Dylan persisted, pointing to my head. "You can't see out of one eye!"

GRRR...

"Look, it's just a fashion thing. You're a boy – you wouldn't understand," Soph told him, without realizing she'd just helped me out of an awkward situation.

('Cause let's face it, it wasn't so much a fashion thing as a hiding-my-half-an-eyebrow thing.)

"Shut up and let Indie talk about her

list, Dylan!" Fee laughed, chucking a Beanie frog at him.

Yes... I wanted to get back to the list, and off the subject of my a-bit-different hairdo and the secret it was hiding.

"Uh, OK," I said quickly, glancing down at my notepad. "The next one is:

❸ You can get a job and live where you want, without your parents.

"What's that about, then?" asked Sophie, looking at me kind of confused.

"I got the idea from Caitlin. Y'know, when she was eighteen, she left her family in Scotland and moved all the way here for her first nannying job!"

"But you *can't* do that, Indie!" said Dylan.

"I can't do what?" I asked, trying to

figure out what he was on about now.

"You *can't* get a job and live wherever you want, 'cause you're only ten!"

"Yes, I know that, but all I'm saying is that it's one of the very cool things about being a grown-up. And someday I'll be able to do it!"

"I wouldn't like to live on my own," said Soph. "Wouldn't it be lonely, not having your mum and dad around?"

"No, it would be very cool," I replied, thinking that I didn't live with my dad anyway, and Mum had been just as annoyingly distracted with me this morning. (She'd even got a bit cross when I said "**Yuck**" as she fed a cricket to the tree frogs...)

"Why?" asked Dylan.

Honestly. What's he like?

"Because … because it just *would*!" I said, feeling like taking the yo-yo out of his hands and strangling him with it.

"No," Dylan said with a shake of his head. "I mean why have you got

'I'M REALLY SNY AND NOBODY NOES IT'

written on your T-shirt? And what does **'SNY'** mean?"

"It's **'SHY'**," I corrected him.

I'd really taken my time copying Caitlin's T-shirt. It didn't look quite as good as her printed one, but I'd made sure I wrote out the words in red fabric pen really neatly. How could Dylan think it said **'SNY'**?!

"You've spelt 'knows' wrong too," Fee pointed out, sticking a finger (and a tiger Beanie) in my direction.

Urgh … how had I managed to do *that*?

"I don't get it, Indie…" muttered Soph, frowning at my top. "You're not shy. And if

you *were* shy, then everyone would know 'cause you've written it on there!"

"It's meant to be funny," I tried to explain. "It's meant to be…"

I couldn't think of the proper, grown-up word for being funny in a sarky way, so I just said "funny" again. Dylan and Soph and Fee stared at me then, making me feel like a total lemon.

Suddenly, something zapped into my brain. Maybe Dylan and Soph and Fee weren't grown-up enough to understand my new project. After all, Dylan was goofing around with a yo-yo, Fee was hugging a bunch of Beanie toys, and Soph didn't get the joke on my T-shirt.

I'm sny
But
nobody
noes
it

49

Or was I just being too hard on my friends?

"HEY," said Soph, glancing around at us all with a grin. "Anyone fancy going to the park and rolling down the hill till we're sick?"

Hmmm,

then again,

I think I was right the first time.

"I'd better go," I said, pulling my hoodie back on and packing my notepad into my bag. "I forgot that I've got stuff to do at home."

Stuff like hanging out with a *proper* grown-up called Caitlin.

(Only I guessed I'd better change my T-shirt. I didn't want Caitlin thinking I was a big kid for copying her...)

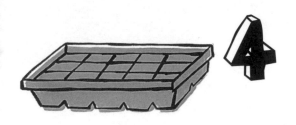

Caitlin does a make-over

Oops.

I'd had a bit of a not-very-grown-up accident on the walk home from Soph's. Something to do with a very big bubblegum bubble going **splat**...

"Where's Mum?" I muttered, bending over at the kitchen sink, with my nose squished flat against the draining board.

Caitlin, meanwhile, was pressing ice cubes down onto my gummed-together clump of hair. (Frozen gum comes off easier than the chewy version, she said.)

I didn't want Mum to see me like this. The funny mood she was in this week, she'd probably end up telling me off again...

"I think Mrs Kidd said there was an emergency at the rescue centre," said Caitlin. "A snake tied itself in a knot or something..."

"Are you *sure?*" I asked, turning my head sideways and frowning at her.

sssssssssssssi

Living with my mum and loving animals (nearly) as much as she did, I couldn't help thinking that it *didn't* sound like the sort of thing a snake would really do.

"Um, or maybe she had a meeting. I can't remember," said Caitlin with a vague shrug. "I was in the middle of didgeridoo practice when she was leaving so I didn't listen properly."

As she talked, I noticed that Caitlin was wearing the MOST amazing make-up. She'd used blue and purple and pink eyeshadow and sort of smudged it prettily together. It reminded me of the school fair last year when I got my face painted as a butterfly.

"I like it. Your make-up, I mean," I told her out

loud, while in my head I added

4 You get to wear amazing clothes and make-up and nobody can say anything

to my **BEING GROWN-UP IS COOL** list.

Caitlin seemed pretty chuffed at the compliment.

"Thanks, kid! I just started a new job today, so I'm making an *extra-special* effort to look nice."

"Oh? Who are you looking after this time?"

It's hard to keep track of the little babies and children that Caitlin looks after, 'cause of her getting fired and starting new jobs all the time.

Actually, the fact that Caitlin gets fired all the time is weird. I don't know why it happens, as she is very cool and nice and everything. When she babysits me, we have a lot of fun.

Sometimes she fixes my hair in mad punk styles.

Sometimes we just sit and watch telly and eat truck-loads of chocolate and Wotsits.

And sometimes we play *really* funny games,

like a brilliant kind of hide-and-seek, where she's a vampire and she's coming to get me.

"I'm looking after a baby called Scarlett," said Caitlin. "She's pretty cute ... but a wee bit shy."

I like Caitlin's Scottish accent, and I like it when she says stuff like "a wee bit" instead of "a little bit".

"Hey," Caitlin said suddenly. "Do you want me to do the same make-up on you?"

"Yes, please!"

And so for the next few minutes I sat very still and silent and let Caitlin concentrate on smudging rainbow colours around my eyes. The only sounds in the house were the doggy snoring of Dibbles,

Kenneth and George, the bubbling of the
fish tank and the **"ribbett, ribbett"**
of three tree frogs.

And then the doorbell joined in.

DING DONG

"I'll get it!" I said, jumping up and racing the dogs to the door, just like I always did.

Yanking the door open, I found Dylan on the doorstep, along with his bike.

"Indie?"

Um, he seemed to be looking at me all funny, as if I was some complete stranger, and not the step-sister he last saw twenty minutes ago at Soph's place.

And how come he said my name like it was a question?

"Yes ... it's me, duh!" I laughed.

"What's up? Do you want to come in?"

"Er,

no...

no,"

he bumbled, backing away from me, which was hard, since Dibbles the dog had waddled out and grabbed the ankle of his jeans for fun.

"Well, how come you're here, Dylan?"

"I was just cycling home, and I wanted to check you were OK. 'Cause you left Soph's really quickly, like you'd gone...

um..."

"Gone what?"

Dylan's eyebrows (all two of them) did a little dance on his forehead, as if he was trying to figure out what to say next.

And then he just came out and said it.

"Gone nuts."

"Dylan! What are you on about?!" I gasped, feeling hurt *and* confused *and* annoyed with him all at once.

"Oh, helloooooooooooooo, Indie!" a voice trilled over the hedge at that precise second.

It was Mrs O'Neill, our nice old lady neighbour from over the road.

I was quite glad to see an adult who spoke sense (ie Mrs O'Neill) instead of a little boy who said stupid things (ie Dylan).

"Hello!" I said cheerfully to Mrs O'Neill.

At the same time,

I noticed Dylan shaking Dibbles off his leg and reversing his bike out of the gate.

He didn't even say bye.

Honestly, what a strange "wee" boy he was (as Caitlin might say).

"Oh! Are you all right, Indie, dear?" Mrs O'Neill suddenly asked, frowning hard at me. "Have you been in an accident?"

"Er, no!" I said with a shake of my head, wondering if she'd gone a little mad. (That wasn't a mad thing to say, by the way – Mrs O'Neill was often out polishing her wheelie bin or dusting her hedge.)

"But then why do you look so … *odd*, Indie dear? And your eyes … aren't they bruised?"

"Um … it's nothing. Honestly," I replied, my heart suddenly beginning to sink. "Listen, I'd better get back to my homework."

With a friendly wave, I quickly shut the door and turned around to look at myself in the hall mirror.

Uh-oh.

Caitlin had been so keen to do my eye make-up that she hadn't finished picking off the hardened bubblegum in my clump of hair. It was now standing straight up at the front of my head, like a fringe in a force 10 gale (with bubblegum in it…).

And if my hair was standing straight up, it meant that Dylan and Mrs O'Neill would be getting a full-on glimpse of my half-an-eyebrow.

And maybe Caitlin's version of the blue, purple and pink butterfly eye make-up looked great on *her*, but I could see that from a distance, it might look like I'd gone three rounds with a kangaroo in boxing gloves.

Oooh, this trying to be grown-up thing was much, MUCH harder work than I'd expected…

Getting Dylan into trouble

> **5** People don't make a fuss when you say you can look after yourself.

I came up with the latest reason for my **'BEING GROWN-UP IS COOL'** list this morning, before I left for school.

Mum had been all flustered and grouchy again. I didn't know what was making her that way, and thought that asking might make her even *more* flustered and grouchy.

So I just tried to be useful and fed the

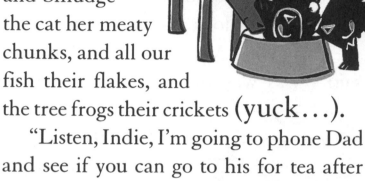

dogs their
crunchies,
and Smudge
the cat her meaty
chunks, and all our
fish their flakes, and
the tree frogs their crickets (yuck...).

"Listen, Indie, I'm going to phone Dad and see if you can go to his for tea after school. I've got to work late at the rescue centre again today, and Caitlin says she won't get back in time to mind you."

Ah, so that was why Mum was stressing. She'd been wondering what to do with me. Not that she needed to do anything with me – I could look after myself for once, *couldn't I?*

And anyway, I didn't want to go to Dad's – at least, I didn't want to go to

Dad's and see Dylan after looking like such a dork in front of him yesterday…

"Mum, I could just come home! I don't need anyone to look after me!" I protested.

That's when Mum made a total fuss and said I was way too young to be left on my own.

Great.

Somehow I managed to convince her that I had lots of homework and wouldn't be able to concentrate at Dad's 'cause of Dylan being there. Could I maybe just go over to Mrs O'Neill's for a couple of hours?

After that fun start to the day *(not)*, I spent the morning at school…

a) **FUMING** at my mum,

b) smoothing hair down across my left eye,

c) only talking to Soph and Fee with the right-hand side of my face (guess why),

AND...

d) realizing (**URGH**) that I should talk to Dylan and 'take him into my confidence'. (Grown-up way of saying I needed to **BEG** him to keep my half-an-eyebrow secret.)

Meet me in park after school?

I'd texted him, as I waited in the school lunch queue for sausages and mash.

He didn't get straight back to me – so by the time I'd got to the pudding section I panicked and sent him a photo-message of my face too. Well, not my face, exactly ... more my left half-an-eyebrow, so that *he* knew *I* knew *he* knew.

If you see what I mean.

OK he'd suddenly texted back. **Where in park? Not beside swings and slide – you might frighten little kids!**

Well, ha, ha, ha, I thought, rolling my eyes.

But Dylan was being *quite* funny, I supposed.

Anyway, here we were in the park: me and my *quite* funny step-brother Dylan.

⑤ People don't make a fuss when you say you can look after yourself.

Dylan mumbled aloud, reading my opened notebook upside down as he sat on the grass next to me. "Is that another reason why

BEING GROWN-UP IS COOL?"

"Yep," I said with a nod. "I came up with that one 'cause Mum doesn't like the idea of me being home alone. Don't know what she thinks I'd do. I'm not a baby – I wouldn't exactly stick my fingers in the sockets or play with matches!"

"Yeah, but maybe you might have an accident or something…" Dylan suggested.

"How much of an accident could you have, sitting on the sofa watching TV and eating biscuits?!" I laughed.

"Dunno."

"But just think about it, Dylan; think how amazing it would be if you said you could

look after yourself and people just went ...
'OK'!"

"Is that important?"

"Well, *course* it is!" I told him. "It would mean people trusted you, and didn't feel like they had to watch over you every single second of the day!"

Dylan blinked very fast, as if his brain was a computer and he was storing information.

It didn't seem like he was planning on saying anything though (Dylan can be a bit odd, in the nicest way), so I decided it was time to tell him why I'd asked him here.

And then a noise got in the way.

Boingggg!! Boingggg!! Boingggg!!

"What is that?" I wondered aloud,

glancing around at the park for signs of **boingggging.**

"My phone," said Dylan, his face clouding over as he stared at the screen.

Only Dylan would have a ring-tone that sounded like Zebedee from *The Magic Roundabout*...

"Aren't you going to answer it?"

"Nope," he replied, shoving it back in his pocket. "It's my mum. I'll speak to her later."

"Uh, all right. Anyway, I wanted to ask a favour. I know I looked freaky yesterday, but I was just fooling around with Caitlin. And about my eyebrow, well—"

Bleep!

Sounded like Dylan had a text message

now. I waited as he took his phone out, frowned again and speed-texted something back.

I thought he might tell me who he was texting, but instead he just looked up and said, "How did you do it?"

I couldn't figure out what Dylan meant (for the zillionth time), and then I sussed it.

"Doesn't matter," I said, smoothing the long bit of hair over my eyebrow. "Dylan, I really need you to PROMISE me that you won't say anything about it to anyone. Specially anyone like Soph and Fee!"

"How come you don't want them to know? Aren't they your best friends?"

"Yes, but they'd *so* tease me if they knew. I mean, even *I* would tease me if I saw my half-an-eyebrow."

Honestly, I couldn't face Soph and Fee taking the mickey out of me, specially since Mum was making me feel bad enough. Last night, she'd smothered 'soothing' cream on my bald bit of eyebrow. The sort of 'soothing' cream you put on babies' bums when they've got nappy rash.

Oh, the shame…

"It won't take long to grow back, I hope," I waffled on, "so it's not like I need to hide my eyebrow for ever or—"

Brrr, Brrrr… Brrrr, Brrrr.

Ah-ha. My more sensible-sounding phone this time.

"Hello?"

"Indie? It's Dad," said my, er, dad.

"Have you heard from Dylan today?"

"Huh?" I huhed, playing for time as I glanced over at my step-brother, and made a sign for him to stay shushed.

"He was *supposed* to be home half an hour ago – Fiona's very worried."

"Oh?"

(More like uh-oh.)

"She tried to get hold of him on his mobile, but all she got back was a very cheeky text, saying that he was old enough to look after himself!"

Oops. Did Dylan do that 'cause of me? Absolutely...

"Really? Oh – I just remembered ... I *did* get a text from him about five minutes ago, saying he was on his way home."

Wow, I was such a lousy actor. Luckily, Dad fell for it.

"Oh, that's a relief. Still, I'll have to have a word with him about texting his mother in that tone of voice…"

"Um, listen, Dad, I've got to go – I'm … with *someone*!"

Blip – I switched the phone off quick before I had to admit that the *someone* was Dylan.

YIKES.

I hadn't thought being a cool grown-up would be quite so complicated, or mean getting my little step-brother in such a huge heap of trouble.

Little did I know I was also about to be in a HUGE heap of trouble myself…

Now it's double trouble

On the way home from the park, I *tried* to take my mind off the trouble I'd got Dylan into, all because of my **BEING GROWN-UP IS COOL** list.

So I thought about tree frogs. And here's what I thought about tree frogs… I might technically be a kid, but I knew TONS about animal stuff that most adults didn't know. Like with tree frogs, I knew that…

a) they originally came from AMERICA and MEXICO (green tree frogs, anyway),
b) they needed to live in a VIVARIUM (posh word for tank),
C) they needed a HEAT LAMP (posh way of saying light bulb),
d) they needed to have their heat-lamped vivarium covered in SPHAGUM MOSS (posh word for just moss) AND
e) they ate crickets (yuck).

The tree frog stuff was rattling around my brain when I turned into our street and saw something that made my stomach do a backflip.

Mrs O'Neill, our old lady neighbour, was standing on the pavement – her nicely dusted hedge behind her – and she was crying…

Mum – who was supposed to be working late today – had her arm around Mrs O'Neill and was giving her a pat on the back with one hand, and pressing her mobile to her ear with the other.

HELP … what was wrong?

I started running towards them, desperate to find out what was going on.

And then – as they both set eyes on me – it dawned on me that *I* was what was going on.

"Indie!!" Mum called out sharply. "Where have you *been*?"

Her face was doing the opposite of smiling.

"The park...?" I told her, in a teeny-tiny voice, realizing I'd forgotten all about Mrs O'Neill minding me.

"Oh, Indie! Thank goodness! You're not dead!" gasped Mrs O'Neill, hurrying towards me in her cosy cardie and slippers and giving me a HUGE head-to-chest hug.

"The *park*?" I vaguely heard Mum say. "Well, you weren't at the park with Soph or Fee, because I just called them! And you *know* you're not allowed to go to the park on your own unless you've got the dogs with you!"

Mrs O'Neill's arms – and cardie – were wrapped around my head so tightly it was hard to hear Mum properly.

"Mmm … I wasn't at the park on my own … I was with Dylan…" I mumbled, not sure if Mum could hear me back.

She could.

"With Dylan? Well, who you *were* or *weren't* with isn't really the point, Indie. The point is, we've been worried *sick* about you! Mrs O'Neill expected you at her house straight after school," I heard Mum rant. "And when you didn't turn up, she had to phone me at work to let me know you'd gone missing. I was just on the verge of phoning your dad, and then the police!"

"The police? But ... you didn't ... have to ... worry! I hadn't ... gone ... missing!" I tried to protest, as Mrs O'Neill hugged me tighter, kissing the top of my head like I was a long-lost cat that had turned up on her doorstep.

"India, you're only ten years old – of course I'm going to worry about you! Especially when you had your mobile switched off!"

As I smothered quietly in Mrs O'Neil's cardie-hug, I realized that I *had* switched it off – in case Dad phoned again trying to track down Dylan.

"Mum, I'm sorry…" I muttered, gently wriggling free of Mrs O'Neill at last.

"Indie, I'm sorry too… I was hoping you could be more grown-up, but I see you can't," said Mum, rubbing her face with both hands and looking miserable. "Look, can you go home, please? Caitlin's just arrived, and I HAVE to get back to work."

Ouch!

Mum's words and tone stung like the prickliest nettles. I knew I'd messed up, but when did she get to be so grouchy with me?

Whatever – I did what I was told and walked towards our house.

And that's when I suddenly thought of my sixth reason why **BEING GROWN-UP IS COOL...**

❻ You don't HAVE to do what you're told.

Mmm,
wouldn't
that
be nice...?

7

Caitlin's not-very-good news

So, I'd scared Mum by being late home.

Then she was so annoyed with me that I got sort of scared too.

About five seconds – and five steps away from Mum – later, that made me come up with my seventh reason why **BEING GROWN-UP IS COOL.**

7 You're not scared of **ANYTHING.**

"Caitlin?" I shouted, as I hurried in through our front door and away from Mum's bad mood.

"Woof!" woofed George.

"*Mee-howlllll!!*" howled Kenneth, doing his excellent impression of a cat.

"Arf!" arfed Dibbles, **thudda-dudda-dudding** his tail on the hall carpet.

"THUMMMMA-RUMMMMA-RUMMMMA..."

The **THUMMMMA-RUMMMMA-RUMMMMING** was coming from Caitlin's room. Walking along the hallway in a tangle of dogs, I called out her name again.

Nothing. She was playing her didgeridoo too loud to hear me.

"THUMMMMA-RUMMMMA-RUMMMMA..."

88

What Caitlin was playing sounded very sad. But then *everything* on the didgeridoo sounds sad. Even *Happy Birthday* sounds pretty gloomy.

I got to her door and tapped on it. The **THUMMMMA-RUMMMMA-RUMMMMING** stopped.

"Come in!" snuffled a voice.

It sounded as if Caitlin had a cold.

Or maybe not.

As soon as I stepped into her room I saw that Caitlin had been crying – so much that her black eyeliner had slithered right the way down her cheeks. (The clutter of rumpled, soggy tissues chucked on the carpet was a bit of a giveaway too.)

"What's wrong?" I asked.

"Oh, Indie – I'm in so

much trouble!" sniffled Caitlin, as she perched on her bed with her didgeridoo clamped between her knees.

"You're in trouble?" I said, as Dibbles nudged me in the back of the knees and pushed his way into the room too. "How come?"

It was horrible seeing Caitlin looking so unhappy, but it kind of made me feel better, knowing that cool grown-ups can get into trouble too.

"My new job," said Caitlin. "I got a warning today and was sent home early. Scarlett's mum says I HAVE to do better or I'll get fired…"

"What did you do wrong?" I asked, moving a mountain of magazines off her bed so I could sit down next to her. (Dibbles immediately sat on them and

thudda-dudda-dudded his tail happily.)

"Nothing!"

"*Nothing?*" I said, thinking that there HAD to be something.

"Well, Scarlett's mum said that babies shouldn't be eating burnt food."

"How did she know the food you gave Scarlett was burnt?" I asked, thinking of the singed sausages and charred beans that Caitlin sometimes made us both for lunch.

"Er ... all her pots were burnt."

I suddenly remembered Mum once laughing and saying that Caitlin was a bit of a magician – she could turn the inside of pots from silver to black in one lunchtime.

Still, Caitlin couldn't be threatened with the sack over a couple of pots that needed scrubbing, could she?

"Was that it? Was that all?" I asked her in surprise.

"No ... she didn't really like the mobile I made and hung up above Scarlett's cot," Caitlin explained, as she rubbed the tears from her face with the back of her hand.

(It smudged the eye-liner even more, so she

92

looked like a picture I'd once seen at school of a Victorian chimney sweep.)

"Why not?"

"It was of bats. She said it would give Scarlett nightmares. But bats are cute, aren't they, Indie?"

"Well, yes … ish," I shrugged. "So you barbecued Scarlett's lunch and made her a mobile her mum didn't like. Is that *all* you did?"

"Yes. Apart from playing dressing-up with Scarlett."

"WHAT did you dress her up as?"

"I only got as far as painting her nails deep purple, same as mine, see?" said Caitlin, wiggling her fingers at me. "That's when Scarlett's mum came in and flipped out."

Yikes. I didn't want to say so in front

of Caitlin, but I could sort of see why Scarlett's mum might be a teeny bit worried…

"The thing is, Indie, if I get fired again, I can't pay your mum rent!" Caitlin added.

"Oh," I muttered.

That didn't sound good. Mum didn't earn bucketloads as Assistant Manager of the rescue centre and *really* needed Caitlin's rent money.

"I don't know what to do!" Caitlin squeaked, and started crying all over again.

The crying seemed to freak Dibbles out – his tail stopped **thudda-dudda-dudding** and he squished down on his fat tummy and crawled under the bed.

The crying sort of freaked me out too, specially since Caitlin was crying with her head on my shoulder.

I froze.

What was I supposed to do?

I hadn't *ever* had an adult do this to me. Adults don't tend to cry and want a cuddle from kids; it's always the other way round.

And then I realized what I *needed* to do.

"There, there," I said in a comforting voice, putting my arm around Caitlin and giving her a squeeze. "Everything will be OK."

I had no idea how things would be OK. But one thing was for sure; taking care of Caitlin suddenly made me feel very grown-up.

Cool…

8

Having a tricky time (or three)

My not-very-grown-up eyebrow disaster happened on Sunday.

It was now five-past-getting-out-of-school time on Wednesday.

So I reckoned that the missing part of my eyebrow *must* have started to grow back.

I lifted up my fringe and checked out my reflection in the newsagent's window.

Urgh ... nothing yet.

I was staring and urghing to myself when two someones ran shouting along the pavement towards me.

"Indie!" shouted one someone, who was Soph.

"We've just had a great idea!" shouted the other someone, who was Fee.

I'd only said bye to them two minutes ago – we weren't going the same way home 'cause I was going to catch the bus to Dad's. (I was having tea there – Mum was working late. Again.)

"What's that, then?" I said, brushing my fringe back in place fast.

"Look – a new doughnut place has opened in the shopping centre!" Fee panted breathlessly, waving a leaflet she must've just been handed.

"Yeah!" nodded Soph. "They've got loads of flavours, like *chocolate glazed with choc chips*—"

"AND *chocolate glazed with chocolate sprinkles!*"

"AND *marshmallow flavour with vanilla frosting!*"

"AND *popcorn flavour with toffee frosting!*"

"AND *peanut butter custard flavour!*"

As Soph and Fee jabbered on, I felt kind of sick. I don't know whether it was the thought of all those tastes mixed together, or the fact that my friends had so *nearly* caught me with my missing eyebrow on show.

"So anyway," said Fee, "why don't we go tomorrow after school and blow all our pocket money on tons of doughnuts!"

For a second, I thought that could be fun, in a silly way.

And then I pictured us all sitting in the shopping centre trying to cram as many doughnuts in our mouths as possible and decided it was just plain silly.

And not a very grown-up thing to do.

"Nah," I said with a shrug. "Don't *really* fancy it."

"Please yourself!" said Soph, looking as surprised as if I'd turned down the chance to win a zillion pounds. "But since you're going to your dad's, can you ask Dylan if he wants to come?"

"Yeah, OK," I nodded at Soph and Fee as I started backing away.

(It was starting to get windy. The last thing I needed was for my fringe to flap up right now – not when I'd got away with my half-an-eyebrow secret so far…)

"Hey, Indie!" Fee called after me. "What were you staring at in the newsagent's window just now?"

"Um … only some magazine that looked … nice," I muttered quickly, saying the first thing that popped into my head. "Got to go or I'll be late!"

Y'know, I'd been looking forward to sitting on the bus on the way to Dad's house, just daydreaming and maybe thinking of brilliant new things to add to my **BEING GROWN-UP IS COOL** list.

Instead, I found myself slouching down in my seat, realizing that Soph and Fee probably didn't believe I was interested in stuff in the shop window at all.

And that's probably because the display in the window was for **TROUT FISHING & YOU** magazine…

Urgh.

Everything to do with Soph and Fee had been a bit tricky today.

FIRST, they'd been dying to know where I was yesterday afternoon, 'cause of my mum phoning them and everything. When I told them I'd been at the park with Dylan, they'd acted a bit hurt that I hadn't invited them too. But hey, I could hardly tell them that I was begging Dylan to keep my half-an-eyebrow secret from them, could I? So I just pretended to be suddenly really interested in doing the maths our teacher Miss Levy had set us. (And that must have seemed VERY weird indeed, since I like maths as much as I like Chinese burns…)

THEN they'd kept asking why I was turning away from them when we were talking. And I could hardly say it was 'cause I was scared they'd get a peek at my hidden half-an-eyebrow … so I fibbed and said I'd slept funny and had a crick in my neck.

And THEN there'd been the business at the shop, when I'd fibbed (again) about the magazine, when all the time I'd—

Oh! There was Caitlin.

My bus was crawling along in High

Street traffic, and I got a good long look at her, kneeling down and smiling in a kind of panicky way at a crying baby (Scarlett, I guessed) in a pushchair.

Y'know, when babies start crying, I think they sometimes forget how to stop. And it looked like baby Scarlett was living up to her name, wailing like crazy and turning tomato red.

I saw Caitlin try to give her a dummy, but baby Scarlett just pushed it away and kept right on wailing.

I saw Caitlin making a floppy-eared toy bunny dance in front of baby

105

Scarlett, but she went right on getting more scarlet.

I saw Caitlin pull a funny (sort of scary) face, where she stretched her mouth out and dragged her eyes down, but baby Scarlett just wailed louder.

I saw Caitlin start to look desperate, then all of a sudden rummage in her bag, as if she'd had a great idea. The bus was speeding up, but I still got a glimpse of Caitlin putting a pair of headphones on Scarlett and pressing a button on her CD player. For a second, Scarlett stopped crying, but I think that was pure shock. 'Cause the next second, she was wailing and crying worse than ever.

Oh dear.

I know music can soothe grumpy

babies, but that tends to be there-there, rock-a-bye-baby, humpty-dumpty sort of music.

Something told me that the very loud rock music that Caitlin kept on her CD player wasn't *exactly* the sort of lullaby that Scarlett's mum would approve of.

Wonder how long it'll be, I thought, till Caitlin gets the sack and becomes my babysitter again…?

Oops, I seem to be invisible

I'd just told Dylan all about everything happening with Caitlin.

> The BURNT BABY FOOD.
>
> The BAT MOBILE.
>
> The PURPLE NAIL VARNISH (on someone who was only a few months old).
>
> The LOUD ROCK MUSIC (listened to by someone who would've probably preferred the Teletubbies theme tune).

The two of us were sitting on the sofa in Dad and Fiona's (and Dylan's) living room, while Fiona (a very good cook) made something amazing for tea, and Dad (getting in Fiona's way, I bet) tried to help.

And Dylan ... well, Dylan was nodding hard at what I was saying. And as he was very smart, in his own weird way,

I was pretty sure that he was about to tell me that Caitlin was – sadly – bound to get the sack very soon.

"That sounds great!" Dylan grinned.

"What – you think Caitlin maybe losing her job would be great?!" I asked, completely confused.

"No, what you were saying before that – about the new doughnut shop! Sounds cool!"

Ah, Dylan … he might be hyper-clever when it came to school stuff, but he was still a little kid deep down.

"Never mind doughnuts … what happened *yesterday* when you got home?" I asked him, glancing over at the living room door to make sure it was still safe to gossip. "Did Dad and Fiona go mad at you? Are they going to be mad at *me*?"

The last bit was worrying me; after all, it was number 5 on my

BEING GROWN-UP IS COOL

list that had got Dylan into trouble in the first place.

"Nothing much …
kind of …
and NO,"
said Dylan,
answering all my questions in
order (I think). "And I didn't tell
them I was with you, or about your list
or anything."

"Um, thanks!" That was pretty nice of Dylan, not to land me in it, I mean. "Are they still mad at you, though?"

"Nah," said Dylan, pulling his neon yo-yo out of his pocket and whirling it around. "Mum said that if I was sorry, and promised not to do it again, then she'd make me banoffi pie for tea."

We went quiet for a second, probably both thinking how nice banoffi pie was.

"D'you want to hear the newest thing I've added to my list?" I finally asked, leaning forward to get my notepad out of my bag. (I'd thought of it on the way from the bus stop to Dad's place.)

crack

"No, it's OK," said Dylan, wincing a bit as his yo-yo cracked him on the shin. "I decided I don't want to be a grown-up any more. It's seems like a LOT of hassle. And nobody makes you banoffi pies when you're a grown-up…"

Huh, so much for Dylan being on my (grown-up) side, I grumbled to myself.

"So, Indie, how's your mum doing?" said Dad, suddenly ambling into the living room and plonking himself down on the sofa beside us.

"She sounded a bit preoccupied when she phoned last night and asked me to have you over."

Preoccupied … that's basically a grown-up word for "not listening". And it was the right word to use – when it came to not listening, Mum was doing plenty of that lately, especially when it came to me.

Still, Dad was pretty easy-going for a grown-up. Maybe he'd listen…

"She's gone WEIRD, Dad," I started to explain.

"WEIRD? Weird, how?" he asked me, leaning over and picking the TV remote off the table.

"Well, like last night. I was trying to talk to her about … things, and she just went 'mmm' and carried on with all this work stuff."

I *didn't* want to tell Dad everything. There was no need for him to know that I'd worried Mum, or that I'd worried Mrs O'Neill, or that I'd been late home 'cause I was hanging out with Dylan. But last night I'd been trying to apologize to Mum about all that, and she'd made me feel like – oops! – I was invisible.

"Mmmm…" Dad nodded.

Great.

Dad was glued to the news, where the presenter was announcing that some big politician bloke had chucked his job or been abducted by aliens or something.

Maybe it was VERY IMPORTANT NEWS and every grown-up around the country was glued to it too.

But all I knew was that I'd been right to write down

❽ People **LISTEN** to you.

on my **BEING GROWN-UP IS COOL** list.
    'Cause they certainly don't listen to you
when you're ten and still a kid and invisible...

10

Is my mum an alien?

When Dad dropped me home, I walked into the kitchen and found Mum stroking a tree frog.

She was doing it *very* delicately, as tree frogs are so small there's not much of them to stroke.

Her gaze might have been loving (to the tree frog, not me), but I spotted she had dark circles of tiredness under her eyes. Did that have something to do with the

fact that I'd seen her light on
late,
late,
late
last night, when I'd tiptoed to the bathroom
for a wee? Had she still been working on
all that secret work of hers in the early
hours of whenever it was?

"Are you cleaning out the vivarium?
Can I help?" I asked, wriggling out of my
jacket.

I wasn't offering to help clean frog poo
just to suck up to Mum – I always help out
with animals in our house, whether they're
our own pooches/pusscat/fish, or whatever
foster pets Mum's brought home.

"No – it's probably quicker if I do it

myself," Mum muttered,
hardly looking up at me.

Sigh...

What are parents like? One minute they're nagging you to help around the house more, then the next, they're making you feel like you're too much of a baby to do anything properly.

Y'know, that was another reason why **BEING GROWN-UP IS COOL**; if you want to,

❾ You don't have to do chores at all.

You know something else?

Back at my dad's, I'd made a joke to myself about that politician on the news being abducted by aliens.

But I was really starting to wonder if my nice, ditzy, cute mum had been

121

whisked away in a spaceship and replaced by a grumpy alien from the planet Bedoinggg, who just *happened* to look a bit like her…

"Indie, can you do me a favour?" she said suddenly, finally glancing my way.

"'Course!" I nodded.

"I have a killer headache — can you go and ask Caitlin to give the didgeridoo a rest?"

With a shrug to say yes, I zoomed off to Caitlin's room, where the usual

THUMMMMA-RUMMMMA-RUMMMMING…

was rumbling away.

I wanted to see Caitlin anyway, and find out how she'd got on at work today, after spying what I'd spied from the bus.

"Er, hello? Can I come in?" I asked, after doing some knock-knock-knocking on her bedroom door.

The **THUMMMMA-RUMMMMA-RUMMMMING** stopped with a sudden squelchy burp sound, and a shaky voice said, "Uh-huh!"

Uh-oh. I had the funniest feeling that Caitlin had got sacked.

Again.

"I got sacked!

Again!!"

she sniffled, as I slunk inside her room.

Caitlin's bed was covered in tissues and empty chocolate wrappers. Her feet were covered with Dibbles' head. He's a dog of little brain, but he must have sniffed some sadness and come to keep Caitlin company.

Either that, or her shoes were just very comfy for a little snooze.

"But why!" I came out with, even though I kind of guessed why.

"I dunno!" sniffed Caitlin, wiping her nose and smudging her purple lipstick at the same time. "I took my didgeridoo along today, and played Scarlett some nursery rhymes when we got back from town!"

"And?"

"And Scarlett's mum walked in right as Scarlett started crying during *Twinkle Twinkle*…"

To a baby, the rumbling vibration of the didgeridoo probably made *Twinkle Twinkle* sound like there was an earthquake happening in the room. Specially after the loud rock music she'd had to listen to in her buggy earlier.

But then I had to sound sympathetic for Caitlin's sake. So I said, "Scarlett's mum sacked you for *that*?"

"Yes … and the games I told her I played with Scarlett today."

"*Which* games did you play?" I asked, wth my heart sinking.

"Just all the stuff *we* do together, Indie! Like pretending to be thunder and lightning by banging pot lids in the dark …

waaaah   waaaah

and Hide and Seek, where I'm the ghost coming to get you … and You're It, when I'm the vampire going to nibble your neck when I catch you!"

As I listened, I thought of *two* somethings.

The *first* something was that Caitlin seemed NOT to have noticed that I was ten years old, and baby Scarlett was about ten months old.

The *second* something was…

"Caitlin, maybe you're not *meant* to be a nanny. Maybe you're meant to be something else!"

"Huh?" snuffled Caitlin, sounding surprised.

"Well, maybe you'd be brilliant at a completely *different* job. Is there anything else you ever wanted to be?"

Caitlin blinked for a second, then nodded hard.

"I always wanted to be the first didgeridoo-playing pop star!" she gushed.

Hmmm.

That sounded very exciting but not very sensible. It's a bit like Ethan Kent in my class who's always going on about being Spider-man when he grows up.

"Cool!" I said aloud to Caitlin. "Listen, I'll go and get some juice and biscuits and we can talk about it some more!"

"OK!" said Caitlin, giving me a watery smile and looking almost cheered up.

As I searched the kitchen cupboards for Hobnobs, my head whirred fast, trying to think of something else interesting – and not mad – that Caitlin could do as a job.

And then it hit me.

OK, *three* things hit me...

1) Mum seemed to be **MADLY** busy at work right now.

2) **Caitlin** was pretty good with animals (though **ANYTHING** small that moved fast tended to freak her out a bit).

3) **Maybe** they needed more staff at the rescue centre and **maybe** Caitlin could work there!

All that thinking was the *easy* part, though. The hard part was suggesting it to the grumpy alien who looked like Mum. That made me sort of nervous.

I glanced over at her, all hunched up over a bunch of bills or something, looking very serious.

It was right then, as I got a

wibble in my tummy, that I remembered

7 You're not scared of **ANYTHING.**

on my **BEING GROWN-UP IS COOL** list. Not being scared of anything sounded like a good idea right now, so I decided to be very grown-up and talk Mum into helping Caitlin.

"Mum…"

"Mmmmm?"

"Caitlin quite fancies work-ing with animals instead of kids," I said, fibbing a *bit* and missing out the part about Caitlin getting sacked again, in case it got Mum annoyed or something.

"Has Caitlin been sacked *again?*" Mum sighed, shooting me a weary look.

"Mmm. A bit," I nodded. "But like I say, she's interested in animals. Could she come to the centre sometime? Like for work experience or something?"

My big hope would be that Caitlin would love the rescue centre and that the animals in the rescue centre would love Caitlin, and the manager would give Caitlin a job on the spot.

I looked pleadingly at Mum, who looked on the verge of sighing a very l - o - n - g sigh and saying "No".

"Sighhhhhhhh,"

sighed Mum. "Well, at least if Caitlin isn't working, it means she could look after you when you come home from school tomorrow. Why don't you both come round to the rescue centre then?"

"Oh, thank you, Mum!" I gasped, forgetting that Mum was an alien and throwing my arms around her.

It was a nice hug, for an alien. It almost felt like the real thing. In fact, it made me *really* miss my human mum…

Caitlin's new career

"How's it going?" asked Mum, bumping into me and Caitlin in the rescue centre reception.

"Great!" I told her.

"Mmm!" mumbled Caitlin.

Well, the last hour had been great for me, but then I love any excuse to come to the centre and hang out with the animals.

I don't think it had been *quite* so great for Caitlin.

"Is that mud?" she'd asked me, when Peppa the pot-bellied pig rubbed against her leg and left an icky brown mark on her trousers.

"Er, yeah … and poo," I'd told her.

She hadn't liked it much when Jenny the goat headbutted her in the bum and sent her flying into a haybale.

And it was a pity that the *one* grumpy puss in the cat-block was the one that Caitlin chose to pat.

("Hello, Mr Tiddles … aren't you— owwwwww!!!")

That's why we were here – the receptionist had gone to get a BIG plaster for the scratch on Caitlin's hand…

So far, there was no sign of Mum's boss, the manager, so there wasn't much chance of Caitlin being offered a job on the spot, like I'd hoped. But as Caitlin didn't exactly seem to be loving the idea of working here as a kennel assistant, maybe that wasn't such a big deal.

"Listen," said Mum, "I just had a word with Amy the vet – she's about to do a procedure, and if you two want to watch, she's fine with it."

"Yes, please!" I said, practically before Mum got to the end of her sentence.

Mum still seemed a bit different or distant or something, but I thought we were getting on better since last night's hug. The fact that she hadn't got annoyed with me for a whole day had helped (yay!).

"Good. Well, put these on," said Mum, shoving white cotton coats our way. "Right, I've got an important meeting to go to..."

"OK!" I said brightly, noticing that

Caitlin was frowning at her white coat like it was the naffest fashion disaster of the decade.

"Oh, Indie!" Mum called out, over her shoulder. "I might not get out of this meeting for a long time. Can you feed the tree frogs for me back at home?"

At last – Mum sounded more like Mum and less like a grumpy alien. She trusted me again! She wasn't treating me like a silly kid!

"No problem!" I told her, feeling very grown-up.

"What's a *procedure*?" Caitlin asked me, reluctantly wriggling into the white coat as I steered her through a couple of swing doors.

139

"An operation," I explained, as we found ourselves in the surgery, where Amy the vet and Jonathan the trainee vet nurse were standing over a table with a small, unconscious dog on it.

Jonathan's job was one I thought Caitlin might like, especially since it *didn't* involve pig poo.

"Hi guys!" said Amy the vet, through her face mask. "If you could watch from over by the wall, to minimize the risk of infection, that'd be great!"

"Is it …

is it …

DEAD?"

whispered Caitlin.

"The dog? No!" I laughed. "They've only anaesthetized it."

I laughed 'cause Caitlin was just joking. Wasn't she?

"Now, Jonathan is going to swab the area to keep it sterile…"

"Swab?" said Caitlin, in a LOUD, non-whispering voice this time.

Oh, that was good – she was looking keen, asking the vet a question.

"Yes, we swab the area with this special liquid to keep it sterile, germ-free," explained Amy, picking up a small silver scalpel. Then it dawned on me that there was something we didn't know.

"Amy, what's today's operation anyway?"

"Oh, quite a simple one. We're going to remove some stones from Ruffles' bladder," said Amy. "We start with a small cut here, like this, and then…"

And then there was a strange

swoooooooooooooooooosh,

142

followed by a
KER-thump

Yikes – Caitlin had just slid down the wall and fainted into a big girl pile on the floor…

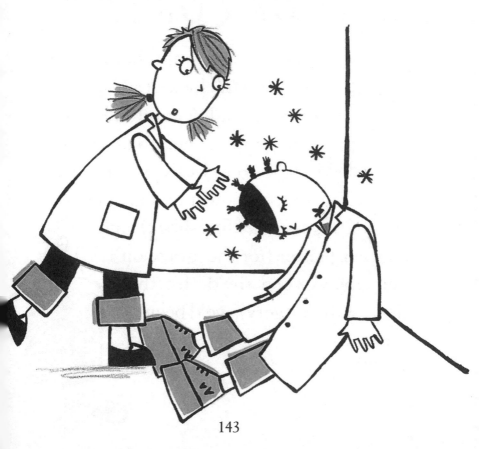

12

Being ten is OK (OK?)

The fresh air on the walk home had helped, but Caitlin *still* looked a bit green.

It was a pity she hadn't mentioned that the sight of blood made her go all funny. Still, she'd come round OK, so once the rescue centre receptionist had given her a cup of sugary tea (for shock) and another plaster (for the graze on her elbow when she'd hit the floor of the surgery), we'd been able to leave.

And right now she was

slumped on a stool in our kitchen, with another cup of sugary tea, blankly watching while I fed the dogs and Smudge – and the tree frogs, of course.

In fact, I was just feeding the tree frogs their crickets (yuck) when a whining noise distracted me.

waaaah

It was distracting Kenneth, George, Dibbles and Smudge too — they all stopped munching their crunchies and crunching their munchies and gazed in the direction of Caitlin.

"Are you OK?" I asked her, worrying that she'd discovered **more** bumps from her fainting fit, or **more** pig poo on her trousers.

"No!" whimpered Caitlin, who was work-ing her way through an entire box of tissues.

"What's wrong?"

"I wish I was ten again!" she sniffled. "I wish I could just sit and watch Scooby-Doo and eat crisps instead of worrying

about work!"

"You're *kidding*!" I said in surprise. "Being ten is no fun – being grown-up is much cooler!"

"No way!"

"Yeah way!!" I insisted, making a grab for my bag and the notebook inside. "Listen to this list I made…"

I started reading it out to Caitlin, but she stopped me by the time I got to reason number 3 of why **BEING GROWN-UP IS COOL**.

"Right, let me look at this properly," she told me, pointing a finger to the top of the list.

And then she began to read it out herself, with extra added bits…

1. You're treated as if you've got a brain.

"Uh, Indie – sometimes I wonder if I have a brain! When you're a grown-up, you still get confused about stuff."

2. People don't tell you off like you're some little kid.

"I still get told off – by the mums and dads I work for!"

3. You can get a job and live where you want, without your parents.

"Sometimes I miss my family back in Scotland so much that it hurts…"

4. You get to wear amazing clothes and make-up and nobody can say anything.

"Indie, when I walk down the street,

148

I get the mickey taken out of me plenty of times!"

5. People don't make a fuss when you say you can look after yourself.

"I've got no one to make a fuss over me. It feels nice if someone cares enough about you to worry…"

6. You don't have to do what you're told.

"But you have to do what you're told at work, or you get fired, like me!"

7. You're not scared of ANYTHING.

"I'm scared of lots of things. I'm scared of the mums and dads I work for, and I'm scared of never getting another job, and I'm scared of the sight of blood, and—"

We didn't get further than number 7 on my list, because *another* thing I knew Caitlin was scared of was small animals that moved fast. So I really didn't want her to notice a tiny tree frog that was hopping dangerously close to her plastered elbow...

boing!

(Why hadn't I closed the tank lid properly? Oh, Caitlin had started whining, that's why.) How was I going to grab the frog and get it back where it belonged without her spotting it and going bananas?

"Hello!" Mum called out from the hall.

Half a second later, she was at the kitchen door-way, in a tangle of licking, welcoming dogs.

"Caitlin, could I have a quick word with you in the living room, please?"

"Mmm!" mumbled Caitlin, looking very, very scared, as if she thought Mum might be about to ask her to move out or something.

boing!
boing!

But
I had
no time
to think
about what
was going on –
I just leapt on the tree frog, scooped it up
in my hand, and let it hop out happily
onto a moss-covered branch in the tank.
It was only when the frog blinked its
tiny eyes at me that I got a chance to let my
mind **whirr.**

And it
whirred
like this…

Even though she didn't get to the end of it, caitlin made my BEING GROWN-UP IS COOL list sound more like BEING GROWN-UP IS A HASSLE. I never thought that grown-ups could be confused or lonely or scared. Maybe being a grown-up was just as much of a pain as being ten, sometimes...

PING!

The ping came from my back pocket. (OK, from my mobile.)

It was a photo message from Dylan – of him, Soph and Fee, holding about a trillion doughnuts up to their mouths and grinning like crazy.

So they **had** gone to the shopping centre together. It was dumb, but suddenly I felt left out...

"Indie?" said Mum, making me jump. "I've just had a chat with Caitlin, and now I've got something to tell you."

I glanced quickly at Caitlin – weirdly, she was looking *really, really* happy for someone who'd just been told to move out.

"I've got a new job," Mum continued. "I'm going to be the manager of the rescue centre!"

"Brilliant!" I beamed at her. Then something suddenly bugged me. "You told Caitlin first, didn't you? How come?"

Wasn't I important enough or grown-up enough to be told first?

"It's not like that, Indie!" Mum smiled, coming over and wrapping her arm round

155

my shoulder. "I've been VERY stressed out the last few days, doing lots of work for lots of meetings and interviews, and I wasn't even sure I could take the job!"

I didn't know what this had to do with telling Caitlin before me, so I stayed silent.

"The hours are going to be a lot longer, so I was worried about how I'd manage, and who'd take care of you," said Mum, touching her forehead to mine. "And then this afternoon, I realized that if Caitlin needed a job, and I was earning more money, then—"

"Then I can look after the house and you, Indie!" Caitlin burst out happily. "That's my NEW job!"

"Anyway, sorry if I've been a bit edgy lately, Indie," said Mum. "I've just had a lot on my mind."

Speaking of minds, mine started **whirring** again.

And it

whirred

like this...

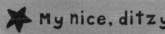

★ My nice, ditzy earth mum is back!

★ caitlin and I are going to have a **GREAT** time together **AND** she'll have time to practise for her career as the world's first didgeridoo-playing pop star!

★ Being grown-up sounds like **pants!**

Who needed all that stressing and worrying? I just wanted to have fun, and I wanted to have fun starting right now.

"So how about sending out for a pizza, and the three of us can celebrate?" Mum suggested, heading over to get the take-away menu from the drawer.

While she did that, I quickly keyed a text message into my mobile.

Got a spare doughnut for yr goofball best m8?

I wrote, and zapped it off to Soph and Fee.

And then I sent Dylan a text that said

Show Soph and Fee this

followed by a nice close-up photo-message of me crossing my eyes, and holding up my fringe so my half-an-eyebrow was on full display.

The thought of Soph and Fee sniggering over my half-an-eyebrow made me snigger too.

And *maybe* we could all go to the doughnut shop on Saturday for a doughnut-eating competition.

And *maybe* we could go the park afterwards and roll down the hill till we were sick.

And *maybe* I'd start to write a new list after that, one called

BEING A KID IS COOL...